Sunspot's Night Out

Adapted by Jordan D. Brown
Based on the screenplay
"Sunspot's Night Out"
written by Joe Purdy

Ready-to-Read

Simon Spotlight
New York   London   Toronto   Sydney   New Delhi

SIMON SPOTLIGHT
An imprint of Simon & Schuster Children's Publishing Division
1230 Avenue of the Americas, New York, New York 10020
This Simon Spotlight edition October 2019
© Copyright 2019 Jet Propulsion, LLC. Ready Jet Go! is a registered trademark of Jet Propulsion, LLC.
All rights reserved, including the right of reproduction in whole or in part in any form.
SIMON SPOTLIGHT, READY-TO-READ, and colophon are registered trademarks of Simon & Schuster, Inc.
For information about special discounts for bulk purchases, please contact Simon & Schuster Special Sales
at 1-866-506-1949 or business@simonandschuster.com.
Manufactured in the United States of America 0819 LAK
2 4 6 8 10 9 7 5 3 1
ISBN 978-1-5344-4919-0 (hc)
ISBN 978-1-5344-4918-3 (pbk)
ISBN 978-1-5344-4920-6 (eBook)

One day in Jet's backyard, Mindy made up a game. She named an animal, and Jet's pet, Sunspot, had to act like it.

"Cow!" Mindy called out.

Sunspot mooed.

"That's amazing, Sunspot!" Sydney said.

Then they heard some strange howling sounds.

"Is that a weird song that Earth people sing?" Jet asked.

"Nope," Sydney said. "That's just some dogs and cats howling."

"That's how they talk to each other," Sean explained.

Sunspot howled too, and pointed to the sky.

"What's he pointing at?"
Mindy asked.
"The North Star," Jet said. "It's always in the same place in the sky. As Earth spins, the North Star looks like it's standing still while the other stars move slowly around it."

"The North Star has been used forever by Earth people to find the direction north," Jet explained. "Long ago, Earth explorers used it when they were traveling around in boats."

Jet's mother called out from the house, "Jet! Sunspot! Time for dinner!"

"Coming, Mom!" Jet called back.

"Let's eat!" Jet's father said.
"Wait, where's Sunspot?" Jet asked.
"Sunspot never misses dinner."
Jet was worried. "Can we go outside
and look for him?"
His father said, "Sure. This food is
still a little frozen."

They went to the backyard and
searched.
"Suuuuuun-spot!" Jet called out.
"Sunspot, where are you?" his
father called out.
Far off they heard dogs and cats
howling. Then they heard a squeak.
"Hey, that's Sunspot's squeak!" Jet
said. He felt a little better.

The other kids ran into the yard. "Where's Sunspot?" Mindy asked. "Maybe Sunspot wanted to howl with the other animals," Sydney said. "Sunspot does have an amazing voice," Jet said. "He sang in the all-animal choir on our home planet, Bortron."

"I hope Sunspot comes back soon," Mindy said.

"Don't worry. He'll come back," Sydney said. "This is where he lives!"

Jet said, "But he's never been away at night."

"Maybe he wants to try being a wild Earth animal," Sydney said.

Jet was really worried. "He doesn't know how to do that. We'd better find him."

"Okay, it's time for Operation Find Sunspot!" Sydney yelled.

"Yes!" the others agreed.

Nearby, a boy named Mitchell was
also looking for an animal—his
dog, Cody.
"I need to track him down,"
Mitchell said.
So he gathered his detective
supplies—his magnifying glass,
his notebook, and dog treats—and
began his search.

At the same time, Jet and his pals searched for Sunspot.

"If only Sunspot left us a clue where to find him," Mindy said.

Just then they heard Sunspot's squeak sound.

"Sunspot's close by!" Mindy said.

Mitchell made a trail of dog treats on the ground.

"I've put dog treats everywhere," he said. "What could be keeping Cody from eating them?"

Mitchell sighed. Where was his furry pal?

The kids heard howling sounds.
"Go this way!" Sean and Jet said,
pointing in opposite directions.
Jet spotted something odd on
the ground.
"Looks like someone dropped a line
of small cookies," he said.

Jet's dad was looking for Sunspot too. He picked up a "cookie" and sniffed it. "I wonder what they taste like," he said.

"Wait!" Sydney shouted. "These are dog treats, not people treats."

Even so, Jet's dad put one in his mouth and chewed.

"Not bad," he said.

"Hmm, you know, Sunspot always goes north when he explores," Jet said.

"Okay, I've got it!" Sean shouted. "To find Sunspot, we need to follow a trail to the North Star!"

"Where is the North Star? Hmm . . . ,"
Sean said.
FACE 9000, Jet's computer friend,
appeared.
"Good evening!" FACE said. "I heard
you say North Star. I'll help you
find it."

FACE explained, "The easiest way to find the North Star is to first find a pattern of stars called the Big Dipper. It's part of a constellation called Ursa Major."

Sydney said, "A constellation is a pattern of stars in the sky."

"Exactly right, Sydney!" said FACE. "When you connect the dots, the Big Dipper kind of looks like a cup with a handle."

"I see it!" Mindy shouted. "It's a *loooong* handle."

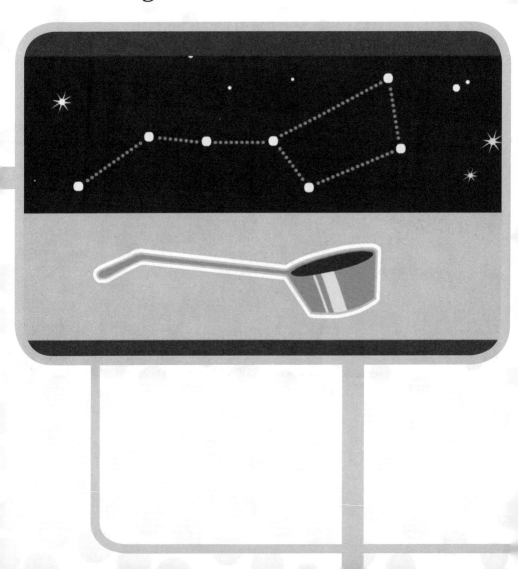

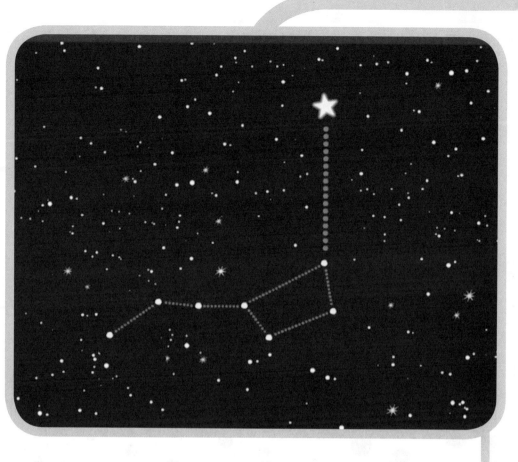

"To find the North Star, follow a straight line from these two stars in the Big Dipper," FACE said. FACE drew a red dotted line to the North Star.

Mindy looked up at the sky.

"But where's the real North Star? Can you help us find it?" she asked.

"Of course!" FACE responded. "Look through me and line up the stars on my screen with the stars in the sky."

"Got it!" Sean said.

Then Sydney connected the dots and pointed up.

"There it is!" she yelled. "The actual North Star!"

"Good work!" FACE said. "Like the
North Star, I'm always around if you
need me. Bye!"
Jet pointed to the North Star.
Keeping his finger in the same
direction, he moved his finger down
near the ground.
"Let's follow the North Star . . . this
way!" he said.

As they followed the North Star, Jet
and the kids heard something move
near a bush.

"What's that?" Sean asked.

Mitchell popped out from behind
the bush. When he saw Jet and
his friends, he screamed,
"Aaaaaaaaah!"

Jet and his friends also screamed,
"Aaaaaaaaaaaah!"

"Mitchell, are you looking for Sunspot too?" Mindy asked.

"No," he answered. "I'm looking for my dog, Cody."

Then they heard more howling. But this time it sounded like music.

The kids followed the musical howling sounds.

Sunspot was using a baton to lead some cats and a dog in a song. It was an animal chorus!

After their song ended, the kids clapped and cheered.

Mitchell looked over at the dog and smiled.

"Cody!" he shouted.

Cody ran over to Mitchell. The kids
went over to Sunspot.

"That was amazing!" Mindy gushed.

"Really awesome!" Sydney added.

"Your conducting skills have gotten
really good," Jet said.

"By the way, Sunspot," Sean said.
"We found you by using the
North Star."
Sunspot pointed at the North Star
and smiled.
Jet hugged Sunspot and said, "I
missed you a lot!"

Everyone went back to Jet's house for a tea party for Sunspot. He was sitting on his special pillow.

"Sunspot, I'm *so* happy you're back!" Mindy said. She gave him a big hug.

"Yeah! Sunspot rules!" the kids cheered.

Later that night Sunspot led his animal chorus again.

In the moonlight all the friends watched as the dogs and cats howled and meowed. They sounded amazing.

Everyone cheered when they were done.

It was a perfect night.

As Sunspot's chorus sang, Sunspot's favorite star, the North Star, twinkled in the night sky.

Read on to find out more about the North Star and constellations in our night sky!

Facts About the North Star

- Polaris is the name for the North Star. It's also known as the Pole Star. The North Star has been guiding us for centuries!
- Polaris is about 434 light-years away from Earth!
- Polaris is about the fiftieth brightest star in our sky. It is also a pulsing star, which means it changes its level of brightness every four days. It's brighter some days than others.

- The North Star is part of the constellation Ursa Minor.
- The North Star is located at the tip of the Little Dipper's handle.
- The North Star is located directly above the North Pole and is in line with the Earth's axis. The Earth's axis is an imaginary line that runs between the North and South Pole through the center of the Earth. The Earth spins on this axis (with a small tilt), which means the North Star appears to stay in the same place in the sky, while other stars appear to spin around it as the Earth turns.

Constellations

- A constellation is a group of stars that form a pattern or picture in the sky.
- There are 88 recognized constellations in our night sky.
- Constellations are used to help astronomers (people who study space), find certain regions in the night sky.
- Not all the constellations are visible at the same time. Some are only visible in the northern or southern hemisphere, while others are affected by the seasons.

Popular Constellations

- **Orion** – Orion can be seen almost anywhere in the world and is shaped like a hunter shooting an arrow.
- **Ursa Major** – Ursa Major means "large bear" in Latin. The Big Dipper is part of this constellation and is used to find the North Star!
- **Ursa Minor** – Ursa Minor is the Little Dipper. Ursa Minor means "small bear" in Latin. The North Star is a part of this constellation.
- **Cassiopeia** – Cassiopeia is known for its unique M or W shape formed by some of the brightest stars in our night sky. This constellation can be seen year-round in the northern hemisphere!

- The zodiac constellations are located within a certain region, called the ecliptic line, in the night sky. This ecliptic line draws out the sun's annual path in the sky. There are thirteen zodiac constellations: Capricorn, Aquarius, Pisces, Aries, Taurus, Gemini, Cancer, Leo, Virgo, Libra, Scorpio, Ophiuchus, and Sagittarius. At certain times of the year, the sun passes through each of these constellations in the sky.

Shooting Stars

Besides spotting constellations, one of the best parts of looking up at the night sky is seeing shooting stars and even a comet once in a while!

- Shooting stars are meteors that burn upon entering the Earth's atmosphere. A meteor is a chunk of rock in space. The trail of dust and gas they leave behind when they enter is what we see streaking through a clear night sky.
- Comets are giant frozen rocks that orbit the sun. When comets approach the sun, they leave behind a trail of dust that can be seen from Earth occasionally.

Can you find any patterns in this piece of the night sky?
If you were naming a constellation, what name would you choose?